ΣGYPTIAN
MYTHOLOGY

ERIN PALMER
ILLUSTRATED BY
MATT FORSYTH

Rourke
Educational Media

rourkeeducationalmedia.com

Before & After Reading Activities

Before Reading:

Building Academic Vocabulary and Background Knowledge

Before reading a book, it is important to tap into what your child or students already know about the topic. This will help them develop their vocabulary, increase their reading comprehension, and make connections across the curriculum.

1. *Look at the cover of the book. What will this book be about?*
2. *What do you already know about the topic?*
3. *Let's study the Table of Contents. What will you learn about in the book's chapters?*
4. *What would you like to learn about this topic? Do you think you might learn about it from this book? Why or why not?*
5. *Use a reading journal to write about your knowledge of this topic. Record what you already know about the topic and what you hope to learn about the topic.*
6. *Read the book.*
7. *In your reading journal, record what you learned about the topic and your response to the book.*
8. *After reading the book complete the activities below.*

Content Area Vocabulary
Read the list. What do these words mean?

achieve
beloved
chaos
creation
devastated
incarnation
philosophy
sacred
symbolized
tombs

After Reading:

Comprehension and Extension Activity

After reading the book, work on the following questions with your child or students in order to check their level of reading comprehension and content mastery.

1. Describe one of the creation stories of ancient Egypt. (Summarize)
2. Why did Set kill Osiris? (Infer)
3. Who was the god of the sky? (Asking Questions)
4. If you could be anyone from Egyptian mythology, who would you choose and why? (Text to Self Connection)
5. What did Egyptians do with their pharaohs after the pharaohs died? (Asking Questions)

Extension Activity

After reading the book, choose an Egyptian god or goddess to learn more about. Find a story about your chosen god or goddess. Then draw your own version of the god or goddess based on the story.

TABLE OF CONTENTS

LOTUS FLOWERS, EGGS, AND CREATION

Myths are stories that show what people believed during different times throughout history. The mythology of ancient Egypt is teeming with the adventures of Egyptian gods and goddesses.

FROM NOTHING TO SOMETHING

Every culture has its own creation myth to explain how the world was formed.

Like all myths, Egyptian mythology begins with the story of **creation**. There are different stories about the beginnings of the universe. Some believed it started with a simple flower.

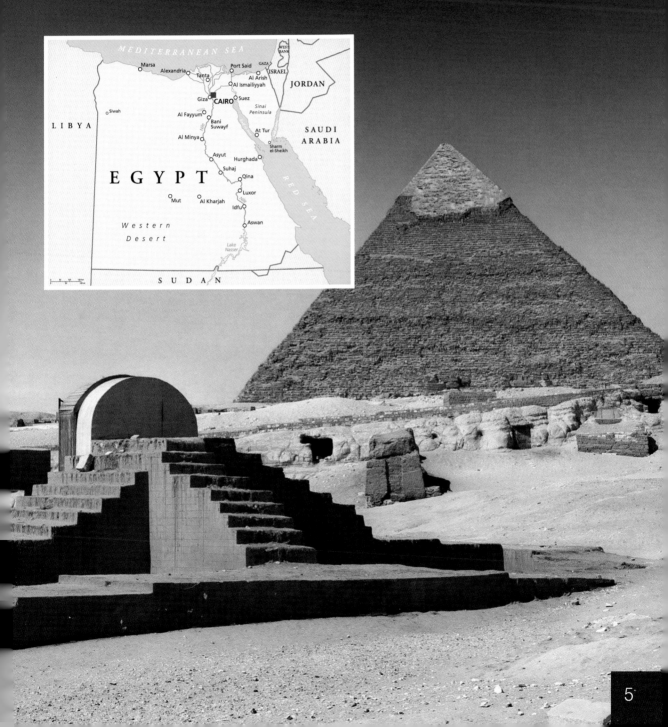

According to the myth, the entire universe was Nun, which means nothing. There was only water, an endless and empty ocean. Then one day a lotus flower appeared with a stretch of dry land beneath it. That land was Egypt.

The sun god appeared from the lotus flower. Some stories said it was the sun god Atum, others said it was the sun god Ra. Either way, the universe began. Because of this story, the lotus flower remained **sacred** to ancient Egyptians.

Sun God Atum

BOW TO THE BEETLE

Ancient Egyptians held many things sacred, including a lot of animals. The scarab beetle was one of their most sacred creatures.

Another creation story began with an egg. This story also started with only an ocean, but this time a single egg was floating in the water. One day the egg hatched and the god Ra was born.

Ra didn't want to just float all alone, so he flew into the air and became the sun god. As the sun, he dried up much of the water on Earth, revealing dry land. He was lonely, so he created himself a wife named Hathor. They had children and grandchildren, which created many new gods and goddesses.

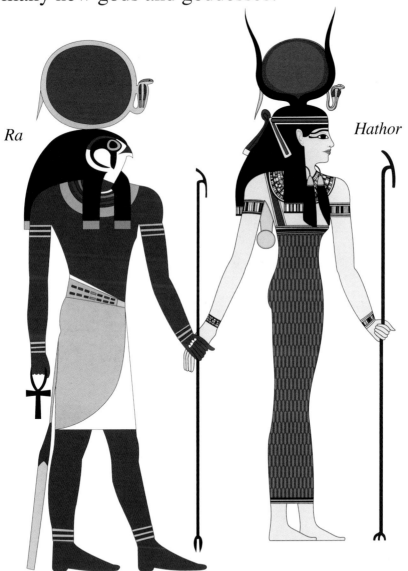

Ra

Hathor

SHIFTING STORIES
Since myths were passed from person to person, the details changed. That's why there are many versions of the myths. For example, some stories say Hathor was Ra's mother.

Osiris, grandson of Ra

Of all his family, Ra had a special connection with his grandson Osiris. That's why he decided to make Osiris the first pharaoh of Egypt. This meant that Osiris ruled Egypt as its leader.

Osiris married Isis and together they were king and queen of Egypt. They had a happy life. But that would soon change thanks to Set, the brother of Osiris.

QUEEN OF THE THRONE

Isis is one of ancient Egypt's most important goddesses. She was also known as Aset, which is translated as "queen of the throne." She was a goddess of childbirth and motherhood. She was thought to be a mighty sorceress. Egyptians believed she knew the secret name of Ra, which gave her tremendous power.

BATTLE OF BROTHERS: SET AND OSIRIS

Set was jealous that his brother Osiris became pharaoh. It seemed unfair to Set that Osiris should rule instead of him. In a rage, Set killed his brother. He chopped Osiris into pieces and threw the pieces into the Nile River.

A GOD BY ANY OTHER NAME

Many of the Egyptian gods had more than one name. Set was sometimes known as Seth.

Isis and Anubis putting Osiris back together

When Isis discovered what happened to her **beloved** husband, she was **devastated**. She found all the pieces of Osiris and brought them to the god Anubis. Anubis was an intelligent god with the head of a jackal. He put the pieces of Osiris back together. In that moment, Isis became pregnant with her son, Horus.

Osiris was back together, but he could not leave the land of the dead. Ra used his powers to create a new position. He made Osiris god of the underworld.

Because Osiris was stuck in the underworld, Set became pharaoh. Isis hid Horus as a child so Set would not murder him. When Horus became an adult, he argued to the court of gods that he, not Set, was the rightful king of Egypt. Set challenged Horus to a series of battles for the throne.

Horus, son of Osiris

Set, brother of Osiris

Horus was god of the sky, war, and hunting. He is portrayed with the head of a falcon.

Some stories say Horus killed Set. Others say Set took the form of a giant snake and hid deep in the forest. Some myths say that the final battle hasn't taken place. When that battle between good and evil happens, Horus will win, and Osiris and the other gods will return to rule Earth again.

Though Isis was thankful that Osiris became god of the underworld, it meant she could never see him again. Since she was immortal, she could never die. That meant she could never go to the land of the dead to be with her husband.

This saddened Isis. So once a year, she would visit the bank of the Nile River and cry. Egyptians believed that when the Nile would rise each year, it was from the tears of Isis.

Isis Temple on the Nile River

KEY OF LIFE

*In ancient Egyptian art, Isis often held a symbol that looked like a key. It was called the ankh and it **symbolized** eternal life.*

GODS, GODDESSES, AND ANIMAL FACES

Ancient Egyptians loved their gods. They worshipped more than 2,000 gods and goddesses. Imagine trying to remember all those names!

Though the Egyptian gods had the bodies of humans, they often had the heads of animals. Here are descriptions of some of the most famous Egyptian gods:

Sekhmet, a daughter of Ra, was the ancient Egyptian goddess of healing. She is also a warrior goddess. Sekhmet is depicted as a lioness, which were considered fierce hunters by Egyptians. She is known as "The Powerful One."

Geb was the god of crops and healing. He was also known as the father of snakes. Ancient Egyptians thought his laughter caused earthquakes. Geb was also thought to weigh the hearts of the dead to judge their souls.

SPITTING IMAGE

Tefnut was the Egyptian goddess of moisture. She was created from Ra's spit!

Bes was the dwarf god of music, art, and childbirth. He was also a war god who protected Ra. Egyptians placed images of Bes above their beds to ward off evil spirits. He was thought to protect women and children above all others.

Bastet, a daughter of Ra, was a feline goddess. She was depicted as a cat or a woman with the head of a cat. She was often painted surrounded by kittens. She could also be ferocious! She was known for killing one of Egypt's deadliest creatures: snakes.

Maat was the goddess of justice, truth, harmony, morality, and order. She was considered the opposite of **chaos** and symbolized the balance of the universe. In the Book of the Dead, the heart weighing ceremony takes place in the Hall of Maat.

MUMMY DEAREST

Mummification took months to complete. Ancient Egyptians believed that preserving bodies this way kept them intact for the afterlife.

CREATOR OF WRITING, THE CALENDAR, AND MORE

According to legend, Thoth created himself. He was intelligent, so he became the god of knowledge and wisdom. He used his smarts to **achieve** a lot of things to help the Egyptian people.

Thoth invented astrology, math and engineering. He created the calendar, science, **philosophy**, religion, writing, and magic. He also invented hieroglyphics, the alphabet that the Egyptians used. Thoth was one busy god!

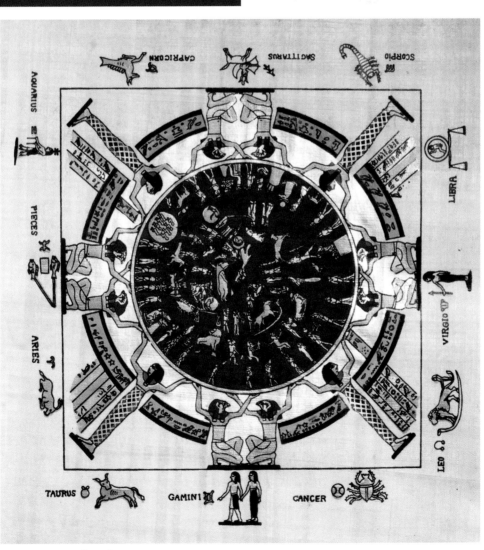

Egyptian calendar

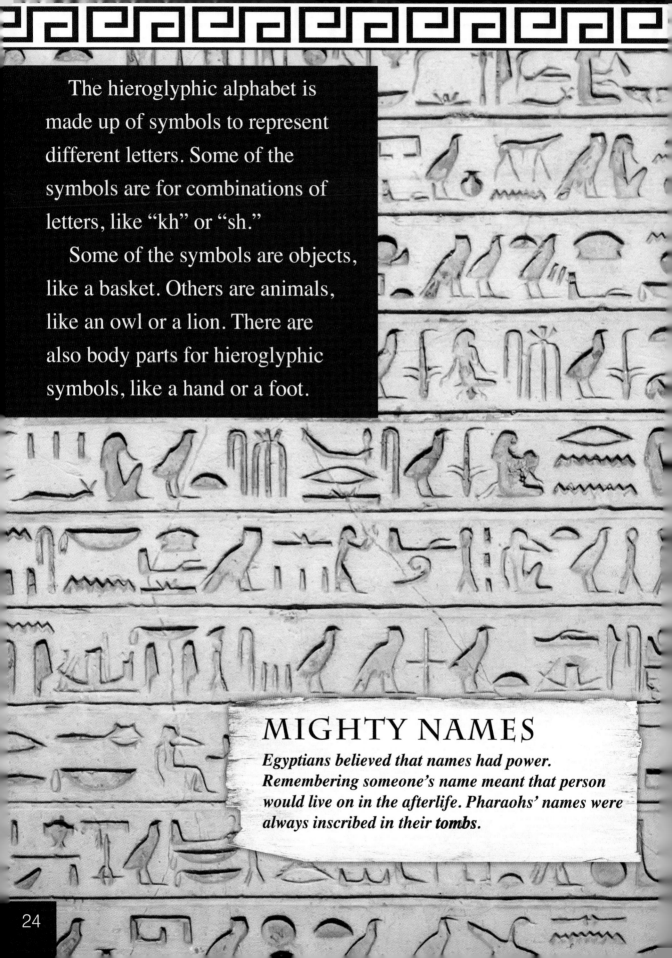

The hieroglyphic alphabet is made up of symbols to represent different letters. Some of the symbols are for combinations of letters, like "kh" or "sh."

Some of the symbols are objects, like a basket. Others are animals, like an owl or a lion. There are also body parts for hieroglyphic symbols, like a hand or a foot.

MIGHTY NAMES

Egyptians believed that names had power. Remembering someone's name meant that person would live on in the afterlife. Pharaohs' names were always inscribed in their tombs.

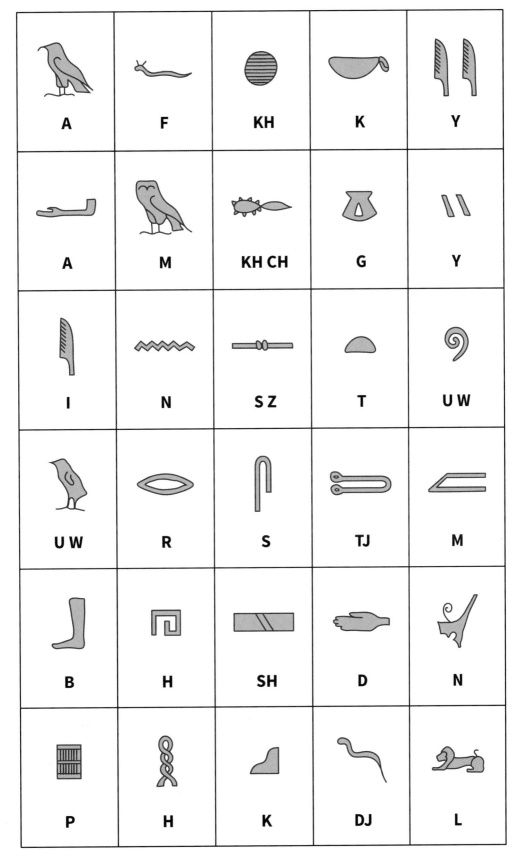

ΣGYPTIAN PHARAOHS: KINGS AND GODS ON ΣARTH

The power of mythology was so strong in ancient Egypt that every pharaoh was considered a god during his time as leader. That's why pharaohs were considered an **incarnation** of Horus when they were alive and Osiris after they died.

Since the Egyptians believed that pharaohs were the connection between their world and the gods, they thought the fate of their land depended on the pharaohs. For this reason, pharaohs were treated to the very best that the people had to offer.

When a pharaoh died, Egyptians believed part of his spirit would stay with his body. That's why pharaohs were mummified and placed in a tomb. Egyptians built pyramids to hold the bodies of their departed pharaohs and their queens.

The pyramid held the mummified body and anything that might be needed in the afterlife: gold, food, furniture, and other offerings.

Visitors to Egypt can still see the power of Egyptian mythology through the pyramids, hieroglyphics, and other historical artifacts that have survived thousands of years.

TOMB ROBBERS

Some of the pyramids still stand today, though a lot of the goods inside were taken by tomb robbers.

GLOSSARY

achieve (uh-CHEEV): to do something successfully after making an effort

beloved (bi-LUHV-id): greatly loved or dear to someone's heart

chaos (KAY-ahs): complete and usually noisy disorder

creation (kree-AY-shuhn): the act of making something

devastated (DEV-uh-stayt-ed): to upset extremely

incarnation (in-kar-NAY-shun): the appearance of a god or spirit in an earthly form

philosophy (fuh-LAH-suh-fee): the study of truth, wisdom, the nature of reality and knowledge

sacred (SAY-krid): holy or having to do with religion

symbolized (SIM-buh-lized): to have stood for or represented something else

tombs (toomz): graves, rooms, or buildings designed to hold a dead body

INDEX

SHOW WHAT YOU KNOW

1. Why was the lotus flower important to ancient Egyptians?
2. Of what was Ra the god?
3. What happened to Set?
4. What did Thoth look like?
5. Why did the ancient Egyptians build pyramids?

WEBSITES TO VISIT

www.egypt.mrdonn.org

www.ngkids.co.uk/history/Ancient-Egypt-Gods

www.historyforkids.net/egyptian-gods.html

ABOUT THE AUTHOR

Erin Palmer is a writer in Tampa, Florida. She loves to read, travel and go to the beach. Erin fell in love with Egyptian mythology after reading a book about it in elementary school.

Meet The Author!
www.meetREMauthors.com

www.rourkeeducationalmedia.com

PHOTO CREDITS: page 3: ©PaulFleet; page 4, 28-29: ©WitR; page 5: ©Peter Hermes Furian; page 6: ©Video-Arr; page 6(b): ©Givaga; page 7: ©marcouliana; page 7(b): ©PSB; page 8: ©Globalpics; page 8 (b): ©Artnata; page 9, 19: ©tan_tan; page 10, 13, 14-15" ©Vuk Kostic; page 17: ©barbun; page 18: ©martrioshka; page 20: ©TerryJLawrence; page 20(b): ©insima; page 23: ©Joselgnaciosoto; page 24: ©swisshippo; page 25: ©Evgenii_Bobrov; page 27: ©Kokhanchiko; page 28: ©AlexVenge

Edited by: Keli Sipperley
Illustrations by: Matt Forsyth
Cover and Interior Layout by: Rhea Magaro-Wallace

Library of Congress PCN Data

Egyptian Mythology / Erin Palmer
 (Mythology Marvels)
  ISBN 978-1-68342-359-1 (hard cover)
  ISBN 978-1-68342-894-7 (soft cover)
  ISBN 978-1-68342-525-0 (e-Book)
Library of Congress Control Number: 2017931270

Rourke Educational Media
Printed in the United States of America,
North Mankato, Minnesota